THE
FOLDINGS

Gordon Kurby

"Two possibilities exist: either we are alone in the Universe or we are not. Both are equally terrifying."

-Arthur C. Clarke

"There is a third possibility. We are holding hands with our future selves."

-Gordon Kurby

Hardcover ISBN: 978-0-9995286-0-0

1st edition, October 2017

Printed in the United States of America

Book design: Crystal Reynolds, crystalink.ca

Wavelength Blue

Blood and wine stains all look the same. The bright white dress shirt has a certain charm when accented with the deep rich cabernet of arterial bleeding. The balm of gracious living, in a universe built on irony, always creates a death tone. Down falls the zigzagging rain ripped by a strong wind, the dirge of a first infant cry flows upward to the angel of time. Fate, dispassionate, tosses men like leaves and litters their lives in outrageous ways. The harvest of destiny's dirty shovel.

There is no heaven, but I want to go there anyway. Therefore, I warn you not to act on the information you shall learn from these pages. I implore you to read no further. I will not be held responsible for menacing your life. In this journey, it is as if we are floating on a skiff beautifully crafted, but the hull is infested already with sea worms. The rot is relentless. Slowly at first, the craft becomes heavier; it can be felt, for she handles in the wind not like before.

Eventually she will sink heedless of all efforts to save her.

You show the galling mirror a piece of your death every day. On this earth we have just four score and ten, the length of men's lives measured a millennium ago. And nothing, not even with our advanced technology, can significantly alter this course. Surviving infancy and if not dashed on the walls of Troy, a man in ancient times could expect to live ninety years. Alchemists in the most modern laboratories and with huge expenditure of society's recourses, with Herculean effort can extend life perhaps to a century. Extend old age? What desperation! In pain a year feels like a decade, hours like days, and minutes an eternity. Extend youth and then you will have my attention...and my sorrow.

Brave men and fools alike have but one way to turn when they are at the far end of the tiller, to control their fate. I say, take risk, heed the call of adventure. Your reward will be unbelievably monstrous waves and a thimbleful of glory. If you do nothing, capricious seas may toss you away from the shoal but only temporarily.

But consider this, I say, be like almost all in this epic: let your sails luff, steer not and drift. You may adorn a commodity called time; it does wear nicely on some. But be forewarned, a fading Marilyn Monroe, her face etched with the acidity of age would bring alkaline tears to mine eyes.

For me, time has no value because it cannot be bought or sold. It does not bear the trustworthy stamp of the smith's mark and the 22 karats. Time is a serpent, a sinister chimera with the sweet serenade of a requiem. The gravity of gold is the only substance on earth that feels not the influence. A singular element, chemically pure that will never lose a molecule of its luster. A type of song that stays in your head, over and over again.

And so, like you, I too was taken in. For the tale told to me by the young conservative esquire on his deathbed is alluring. And it was fortunate for him that "La mort nous acquitte de toutes nos obligations" —death pays all debts. For the man owed me a king's ransom in my personal grief he directly pinged out to others and hence my soul. Such camp robbers do not fare well in this epic, even if they claim to be immortal vampires with great knowledge.

Careful now, for the story he related as payment has wrecked the lives of so many including my own. But with a twisted joy I say you shall soon join us all. For you are much like how he was. You share the same traits. Like you, he was a copious reader. Before his demise, like you, he fully understood that knowledge is rarely declined if it is easily obtained.

Therefore, I can make you only two promises. The treasure still lies intact despite his best efforts. For I have seen it with my own eyes, and ask me not of the location, nor the method per se, as it is lost to me. Perhaps one day, I shall find both. But as for now, my body is broken pieces that no one will put back together. I am in sinuous reality, living under the illusion that my corpse lies on a glacier in eastern Alaska. And that this, what I am about to relay to you, is the vaporous ether of my last thoughts swirling around my facedown body.

Since you have disregarded my warnings and have decided to continue by reading on, your gold cufflinks (oh the wondrous gold!) have just rattled on the wooden tiller. A small twitch of your wrist has unexpectedly steered your skiff and humanities two points to starboard. The monstrous waves, the terror all lie dead ahead. Consider this a personal invitation, for you are now invited to the party. It's all black ties and white shirts and formal dresses. Leave your righteousness at home, keep your wits about you. And please try not to spill too much of your red wine on that perfectly imagined white linen of yours.

Oh, the second promise?

Wavelength Red

E=-T (1)

This unexpected energy of time waves explains

The ignition of stars

The spark of life

The formation of sentient life

The seamless transference of closely related geometric forms of the cosmos from one geometric shape to another to enhance data storage

It is now a whole new ballgame

THE FOLDINGS

Fingers and Toes

Fingers and Toes

"Tag, you're it."

"That's all he said before he committed suicide? Sitting in the chair in your office right in front of you?"

The older, bookish looking man in a neat suit, with glasses that gave him the appearance of a professor, turned his head to the side and stared off, as if considering. The young man interviewing him from across a worn metal desk simply waited for an answer out of courtesy. The older man took off his glasses, held them up to the light, and reluctantly accepting the vision quality, put them back on the bridge of his nose, adjusted them slightly, and turned to face the young man. After a short pause, he answered the question with care.

"He said specifically and exactly these words, "You're it, with no tag backs."

"Like a child's game?"

"Quite so."

The interview room fell silent. There was one window with ornate Spanish style gratings, one painting, two professionals, and three chairs. The steel gray desk between them seemed almost invisible. On the top of the metal desk was a stack of five folders, almost a subset of the tabletop off to one corner. The top file was labeled, "Tom Hastings."

The young man said kindly, "Tom, we know that this profession involves certain risks. One of those risks is a small percentage of the people we treat for depression will commit suicide or will attempt to do so. You have been trained extensively, as have I, on how to handle this, because it is inevitable. Especially if a career in psychotherapy spans any great amount of time."

The young man reached over, and picked up the top folder; he opened it casually and scanned the contents briefly. He then placed this file away from the others and centered it almost in the middle of the tabletop.

"And in your case we are talking about decades, almost a half century of practicing the art of healing others. This is an unfortunate occurrence and nothing more. All doctors lose patients; it is inevitable."

"I had diagnosed him as schizophrenic unspecified."

"Go on."

"The appointment list was nothing special nor was the day. He was a referral diagnosed as a severe cerebral narcissist from Kevin Sholtey. You knew Kevin, didn't you? Well, in any event, he believed narcissists are untreatable as do many in our profession. I beg to differ, as do many, and accepted the referral. That was my first interview with the time traveler."

"Excuse me, Tom, I would prefer we don't use that term time traveler just yet. He was your client or your patient or your charge or however you may wish to describe him other than the fanciful, what we both know to be the imaginary. We can certainly revisit this sequence in your own way, in your own time, but for right now I would recommend we keep it clinical."

"I had prescribed the standard thorazine dose of course, fifty milligrams twice daily."

"May I ask you a question about your mother?"

"You may not."

The two professionals simply stared at each other. They had been schooled on communication theory to perfection with years in a classroom and then in clinical practice. They could never fool each other. They were actors, acting together. Stalemated and both aware of this, and there was safety in that, ultimately for the both of them.

The young man leaned back and laughed heartily at these complexities.

"Okay, Tom, you just go ahead and tell me what happened."

As the story was told, it seemed a simple case, clinically speaking. Akin to a flight instructor with a new student, or an advanced yoga class welcoming an inexperienced member.

The day had indeed been nothing special. Slightly sunny, slightly warm, the traffic had been light. The standard San Diego day, the Spanish style architecture interspersed with glass high rises. His practice was located in the upscale neighborhood of La Jolla. A bright white stucco building with blood red tiled roofs and the correspondingly high rents. The fee for an hour and a half of treatment would buy a major household appliance.

His client had sat down and said very openly, "I am a time traveler."

Dr. Tom Hastings had of course heard it all before and then some. He didn't miss a beat.

"That sounds like a most unusual occupation; why don't you tell me about it?"

He then gave his most fatherly look with a slight, encouraging nod, a look he had practiced in the mirror to perfection when he had been in medical school.

The client then had begun to speak very rapidly, nervously, like he needed to remove a great weight.

"No, that's not exactly right, I have come in close contact with a time traveler, and that's a more precise description. And therefore, using Einstein's field equations and with the theory of observational wave collapse I have observed the phenomena of time travel. I am now forced to time travel in concert with the primary as a type of biological navigational point."

The man's face took on a frown, but he continued without stopping, if anything speaking even more rapidly.

"Also and clearly let it be known, without my consent, in a secondary way, and this is beyond my willpower and beyond my understanding of the natural world. I had nothing to do with the Second World War, but they attempted to hunt the time traveler down and lots of people died behind barbed wire because of it, and I am not responsible for all those civilians that were killed or all those soldiers, either."

The man abruptly stopped talking, a scared and haunted look on his face, his eyes wide and pleading.

"Should I call you William or do you go by Bill?"

The client seemed confused, his face softened with the deliberate distraction, and he said softly, "My friends call me Bill, so I guess that's what we should use."

Dr. Tom Hastings then gave his most approving fatherly look, one where his blue eyes actually sparkled with admiration. Just like seeing his son hit his first home run.

"Bill, let me tell you my initial impressions. Anyone else comes in talking about time travel and it says something. I see from the personal background sheet my assistant asked you to fill out that you earned your Ph.D. in theoretical physics from Boston College. What year was that? No matter, such a great accomplishment, well, this does say something else altogether."

Dr. Hastings added a practiced look to show a slight amount of worry. He did this by raising one eyebrow questioningly while leaning slightly forward in his chair.

"Sometimes when we become expert in a particular field—it can be anything really—we feel that we are superior to all others. It's a belief system that is built over time, but it is reinforced because we really do know more than everyone else in that area of expertise, as you have clearly demonstrated in your chosen field. You are to be congratulated for your superior achievements."

Dr. Hastings then studied his patient carefully. He had laid a trap. For all narcissists need constant reinforcement of their perceived superiority. The reaction to his overblown congratulations would aid in the clinical diagnosis. Bill should light up, look superior, and begin to reinforce his superiority in this case with a medical doctor by throwing into the discussion mathematics so advanced that Dr. Hastings would have no idea what they were.

"All I can say is my physics degree is worthless, I am a total idiot, and the only thing I do know for sure is that I am scared shitless."

Dr. Hastings considered a moment. His face had an unpracticed expression of true worry with deep furrows ripping across his forehead. He said seriously, "I want you to tell me about time travel. Not what the movies say or the fictional books. Explain to me what you actually know."

Bill looked down at his hands a moment and then stared hard right into the eyes of Dr. Hastings. "Are you sure you want to know?"

"If you want me to help you, then yes."

Bill gave the doctor a curious look and then as if deciding the question of free will, he began explaining the development of time travel, the mathematical equations and how they were developed.

"Kurt Gödel was Einstein's best friend. They would go on daily walks together while they were at Princeton. Einstein had remarked that the only reason he got up in the morning was his daily walks with Gödel. They were both Germans from an outsider's relative position. Gödel was actually Austrian. Still this no doubt brought a type of camaraderie. Bill then looked at Dr. Hastings and added, "Gödel was totally insane."

"Is that your own opinion?"

"He believed that ghosts were manipulating his life, that ultimately they were trying to kill him."

"He was completely convinced of this delusion. Specifically, that he was going to die from poisoning. Almost as if he had foreseen his own death."

"Certainly this would be symptomatic of psychological disturbances, but this is not insanity, clinically speaking."

Bill, although a young man, appeared tired and looked older than his years.

"Because of this belief he ultimately would eat only food he prepared himself. He began losing weight and would touch nothing unless tracked with documentable sources of supply. He was finally reduced to eating homemade baby food, all to thwart the foretold belief that his end would be death by poisoning." Bill paused and added, "The last two years of his life were spent in an insane asylum."

Dr. Hastings asked, "And this is important to time travel because...."

"Because he gave to his friend, probably his only friend, during those pleasant walks, a solution. He gave to Einstein a mathematical statement to one of his most difficult field equations. That specific equation demonstrated that time travel was possible. And let me say this as clearly as possible, that Gödel produced a perfect solution to a field equation, and that statement has meaning."

Dr. Hastings looked a bit amused, "Well then, why are we not all time traveling? This Gödel fellow, his name is Gödel, right? Well this esteemed scientist, why is he not a household name?"

"His model requires a rotating universe. That is not observationally confirmed. The last days of his life he would ask over and over, Have they proven yet the universe is spinning? And every day they would tell him no. His last words on his deathbed were specifically asking if humans had made the discovery yet, and the last words he heard in response...."

"No, they have not. So it is not possible, it is just a fanciful idea."

"The universe is changing shape, from our perspective, and rotating at large. There are two levels of symmetry happening at the same instant. It will be proven one day."

THE FOLDINGS

"I see."

Bill began talking rapidly again, losing any sort of cadence.

"It's about information flow. It's about singularities. It's about...."

He went on for five minutes straight without so much as taking a deep breath. He finally finished with what could only be described clinically as a type of verbal spasm.

Bill then stared back at Dr. Tom Hastings wild eyed, but this time the pleading was gone; there was a look of blind panic. He had a small amount of spittle on the side of his mouth, and he was working his jaw back and forth unconsciously as if he were still talking, but no words were coming out. To the doctor he was akin to a frothing riderless horse, galloping recklessly while being chased by wolves.

"Tom, I have to interrupt here. When did you officially change the diagnosis from cerebral narcissism to schizophrenia?" The young man picked up the plain folder, opened it, and began imperially to scan the data, rapidly turning pages.

"What? Are you questioning whether I made a correct clinical observation? Are you therefore doubting my ability to make a diagnosis? Is that what is going on here?"

Dr. Tom Hastings was angry. He had never heard of such a thing. His credentials were impeccable; he didn't need this little snot nosed kid, just out of medical school and less than half his age, to even suggest such an outrage.

The young man looked concerned and a bit sad at the same time. He immediately placed the folder down on the desk, but this time it was off center. His face displayed the type of emotion he would have experienced if he had accidentally hit a cat with a skidding car on a dark and stormy night.

Before speaking the young man softened his voice so it would be only slightly above a whisper. He said with real sorrow, "Oh, I would never do that, of course not." He paused briefly and with deep and genuine earnestness added, "Tom, I have nothing but the greatest respect for you as a doctor with a long and illustrious career."

The young man then leaned back, his face displaying deep furrows like he was suffering from some sort of internal condition and the pain meds were starting to wear off.

Dr. Tom Hastings was breathing hard. His blue eyes were tiny fierce diodes of intensity, beads of malice boring into the insolent young man. Nothing was said by either for some time. They both adhered to the psychotherapy axiom that whoever spoke first in this type of situation lost.

After several minutes, Dr. Hastings breathing began to slow, his anger subsiding. He finally said simply and with disdain, "May I continue?"

"Please do, if you're ready and at your own rate."

Dr. Tom Hastings then did something surprising and completely unexpected. He said with a wry smile, "At times like this I like to flip people off and I do it just like this."

He held up his right hand in the known gesture, but the doctors hand was mangled with one finger amputated altogether. An imperfect message at best.

"I lost my finger and part of my hand when I was a young boy in the gears of my minibike." His smile was wide, almost devilish.

The young man leaned back and laughed heartily, "So no one knows what to think. Oh that is priceless; that's positively rich. Do you use that in traffic?"

"All the time."

"I wish I could do that. Look here, I'm one of those rare individuals with six toes on my right foot. One in a million, see here I must have specially made shoes, and they cost a bloody fortune." The young man smiling, held out from the side of the desk his right foot with a super wide, custom made black wingtip.

"Imagine if you had more fingers on one hand and fewer on the other."

They both laughed together, seeing a camaraderie in being the same, by being different from everyone else, each in his own way.

"No one would know what to think, chaos theory would rule."

"Macro de-coherence."

They both fell into silence, this time an easy one.

Dr. Hastings face turned somewhat serious as he began again.

"The diagnosis shifted when Bill told me about his therapy with Kevin Sholtey. His referral. I was left with no choice but to conclude I was dealing with a deeply disturbed individual. When I learned what went on in those sessions was the moment in time that I realized that this would be the most difficult case in my career."

"Didn't Kevin Sholtey warn you? He must have given you at least a consulting phone call, considering the severe nature and the extent of the mental disease."

"Kevin Sholtey died the week before the referral. All I had to go by were roughed in notes, sent on by his devastated secretary."

"I didn't know." The young man paused and wrote a note in the file. "What in the world went wrong with his treatment? What did Kevin Sholtey do to the man, or worse, what didn't he do?"

"Well, of course the patient would be of little help. Asking anything beyond the simplest of perceptions is even pushing the line. Much like asking someone to describe what their surgeon was like, or how or why the appendix operation went wrong. The patient's knowledge by definition is perfunctory."

Dr. Hastings paused and then continued in a dreamy way, looking off into the distance over the young man's shoulder, not wanting to look the man in the eye.

"Dr. Sholtey's notes were useful in a way. They started out with very precise handwriting, so much so, I marveled at the small perfect cursive. Unusual coming from a doctor's hand. Then about halfway throughout the manuscript, for that really is what it was, or better yet a diary, about halfway chronologically his writing became larger, less fluid. The last few pages were unreadable, as if written by a small child."

The young man considered this and asked a human curiosity question.

"I heard he died in a car accident."

"The police interviewed his wife, and she claimed he had been acting oddly for several days before the crash. She said her husband would roll dice to determine all his actions. Even on the simplest of questions, like if he wanted tea or coffee in the morning. She thought he was joking around, as was his nature. Then for no discernible reason he rented a car from Twopence Motors. The GPS reconstruction showed his route was considered completely random. Multiple U-turns, rapid stops and go's. The authorities determined he was acting in a reckless manner, and they officially labeled the cause of death as "distracted driving."

"How did he crash, I mean how did it end?"

"After several hours of driving aimlessly around the city he finally came to a crossing gate that apparently had malfunctioned. He obviously hadn't noticed, and his car was hit by a speeding train."

"That sounds horrible."

"They say there was one die clutched in each of his lifeless hands."

"Well, that is indeed reckless driving to me. It's amazing how people, even educated doctors, will sometimes bring chaos upon themselves."

Dr. Hastings ignored this completely and continued unabated. "Sholtey had written that he believed the patient, ultimately my client, Bill, had begun working the therapy sessions to his advantage. At the end he was saying that very clearly, that he had been selected and was being used like a piece that needed to be fit into some sort of cosmic puzzle."

The young man scoffed at this suggestion. "Of course some patients, especially a cerebral narcissist, will attempt to usurp the therapy process. We are all trained on how to handle this sort of thing, quite easily I might add."

"No, this was different." But Dr. Hastings did not elaborate further and sat silently staring out the window.

"Let's get back to your sessions with Bill, as that certainly is on firmer ground."

"My sessions with Bill ended with him shooting himself in the head while sitting in a chair having a pleasant conversation. Is there really anything else needed? This, all of this, is absolutely useless." Doctor Hastings waved his arm around the office disgustedly.

"Humor me then."

"Ultimately it was about the death fear. He said the time traveler had shown him his own demise."

"Why would a time traveler do that?"

"Apparently it is necessary to maintain a type of symmetry."

"Bill told you he was not the time traveler, but that he was being used for...what was it? Oh yes, a navigational point."

"Correct. He was an unwilling participant but freely said he would rather have the knowledge than go back to a state of ignorance."

"Tom, I have to openly say, and this is off topic as we are losing the focus of your patient and his therapy, but I am curious. How is it if you could be shown your own death by a time traveler, why you couldn't prevent it in the first place?"

Dr. Hastings nodded agreement, but he also had a ready answer. "Because everything that is done may lead to the exact outcome that is so dreaded. Take the scientist Kurt Gödel for instance."

"Yes, he was constantly on guard so he would not be poisoned."

"And that landed him in a mental institution, where the food preparation in those days may inadvertently have carried a pathogen, not uncommon, and ultimately may have caused...."

"Him to be poisoned to death."

"Precisely."

The young man had waited for this moment. He opened the folder and took out an official looking document.

"This is a police report on the suicide of William Brown, the patient we have been calling Bill." The young man paused a moment for theatrical effect and then continued briskly. "The same patient you have described as a brilliant physicist from Boston College... agreed?"

The young man looked hard at Dr. Hastings and said flatly, "He was a shoe salesman from Des Moines. Do you understand what this means? He was not a scientist; he was not a time traveler."

Dr. Hastings said, "From your relative position in space-time he was indeed a shoe salesman, but only in this epic." The young man just stared with stark disbelief.

Dr. Hastings added with disdain and a grand dismissive wave of his hand, "From my position he was from the far future, probably not even born yet. A brilliant physicist who no doubt became aware of his death in my office in his future time, perhaps even by your scribing the event with those silly notes of yours in that file. That may be all that survived what must be some horrific future human catastrophe. So he learned that he would die in my office after being forced to travel back in history as a biological marker. He probably became a shoe salesman in a vain attempt to bide his time. Perhaps he was delusional and held a false perception that a simple life would protect him or at least grant him temporary safety. Finally one day, no doubt after a series of other very telling events, he must have decided for himself and asked why resist fate? Ironically, he would not be able to halt even his own inevitable suicide."

The young man leaned back and sighed heavily. He seemed to be at a complete loss.

Dr. Hastings picked up on this of course and with a bit of frustration continued. In a twisted form of sympathy he wanted to briefly educate the young man.

"Look, thinking about time travel is not easy, with the sequence of things all badly muddled up and the multiple paradoxes. If it's easier to look at everything happening simultaneously, that's not how it is, but well, that would be a start anyway."

The young man's mouth was open in a sort of frozen disbelief. Not knowing how to respond he was shaking his head slowly without saying a word.

With a slightly higher pitch in his voice, a voice now lined with nervousness, Dr. Hastings said, "If you time travel at some point in the future to the past and die there, you could be shown that death in the historical record of today, before you begin the trip in the first place." He then added, "Agreed?"

The young man, with a look of intense worry, was starting to make notations in the file and simply was no longer paying attention. He said aloud but was talking only to himself, "Such an illustrious career. Such a pity."

As if not hearing any of this Dr. Hastings began speaking even more rapidly. "If the primary time traveler needs biologicals to mark points in time, that's not the way I would build the universe, but no one asked me. And if the secondary time travelers need to see the manner of their own deaths because of symmetry, like the wings on a butterfly, well there you go. I have seen the manner of my own death in the far past, and you will, too. Little hints at first and then the door knocker, the one where the grim reaper is all smiles at the joke, and it all comes crashing down. Mortality, the afterlife, the meaning of life, free will, all of it crashing down like a ton of bricks."

Hastings had a manic look, his hair disheveled from thrashing in his chair while he had been shouting away. Suddenly he stood up, knocking the chair over, still yelling and waving his club-like hand menacingly.

The young man was fearful, frantically pushing a black button on the underside of the desk.

"You little snot nosed pipsqueak, you think you have any idea about the complexities? Of the universe itself?"

Just then the metal door flew open and two powerfully built men dressed in white began to subdue and drag Dr. Tom Hastings kicking and screaming from the room.

From the hall the young man could hear manic laughter and the words over and over, "You're it with no tag backs. You're it with no tag backs." Just like a child playing on a school yard.

Aftermath

The curator for the San Diego Science Museum got the emergency text while on his lunch break. He was at home and headed back to the museum double time. Just as he arrived an ambulance being followed by a police car pulled out. He hurried to the public safety area of the complex and swung open the door.

His staff was all there, along with a couple of EMTs and a police officer. They saw the look on his face and said immediately, "It's over, don't worry."

The group fell silent as they clearly had been shaken up by the experience. In this day and age, almost anything could happen. One of the security guards, a woman, said, "The screams were terrible, I could hear them from the far side of the museum echoing through the halls."

An EMT announced to the room, "I have never had to pry someone's hands off a railing like that. He just wouldn't let go."

Another security guard said, "Just another nut cake losing it. I will admit those body casts are creepy. I mean, to think that's where someone was, and then the lava and ash encased them, and you can see how they were writhing in pain when it happened. Honestly, it is a bit of a gory display. But to go nuts like that and just keep screaming uncontrollably. That guy was psycho." There were silent nods of agreement.

The curator asked, "Where did he go off the deep end?"

"Oh, in the Pompeii exhibit. He was latched onto the railing yelling away, "I'm not it," or something like that. In front of the display with the human casting of some poor devil that got roasted and encased in ash in early Roman times. What was its designation? How did those archeologists describe that one...yes, now I remember.... The man with six toes."

.

The Universe Is Waiting
for Vinnie

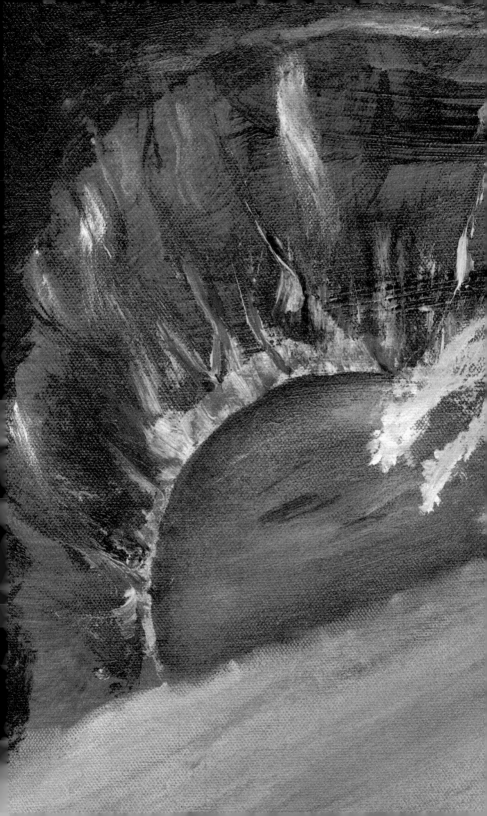

The Universe is Waiting
for Vinnie

The ancient courthouse was large and marbled and mostly vacant. The gold had played out long ago, as had most of the people with their newspapers, the saloons, poetry clubs, all of it. Of course, it was still a town, such as it was, like a hive where the queen had departed leaving dazed and confused worker bees.

"Vinnie." The man who said he was from Jersey was the young lawyer's first client. This was to be his first filing of a legal action in his young legal life. Vinnie had agreed to the hourly and on top of that would buy a first-class plane ticket to a major airport, then a seat on a small turboprop to a regional airport, and then a place on a single engine chartered Cessna to a grass airstrip. Vinnie Russo explained the town was very remote, but the good news was the county airport was walking distance to the courthouse. That was just as well as there were no rental cars available anywhere.

The most obvious question was, "Why do you want me to fly to a nowhere town in the middle of nowhere USA?"

The answer was the simplest possible: "Because they will have to appear right there in nowhere USA to counter the action, and if they don't appear, as is their choice, we will win by default."

The young lawyer ascended the courthouse steps, a satchel under his arm brimming with papers. He dropped his tablet computer, picked the device up, and continued through and into the ornate vestibule.

The county clerk for the court was devouring a giant cinnamon roll. He was a smallish man with a mustache out of the 1980s, who looked something like the character in a detective show in Hawaii.

"Filings are only between the hours of three and four p.m." The man's voice was muffled by a combination of artificial sweeteners, genetically enhanced grains, and a touch of God knows what else. The clock, an ancient looking bronze contraption at least thirty feet above the colonnaded hall showed the time to be 2:58 p.m. The clerk looked up at the clock confirming his correct notation of the time, and then took another giant bite of his cinnamon roll. The young lawyer then watched the man for the next very long two minutes, consuming his snack. The giant bronze clock chimed and the man, wiping his mouth with a cheap napkin, said officially, "How may I help you?"

The lawyer, who had never done this before in his short legal life, said, "I wish to file a lawsuit."

The clerk said with a bored expression, "Type."

This caused some hesitation. The law school had always said a filing was, well, simply fil-ing.

"I don't know."

"Then I cannot accept your legal assertions."

"My legal what?"

"Assertions."

There then was an awkward silence.

"You cannot file unless your intentions are clearly stated."

"Intentions?"

Suddenly a legal lightbulb went off in the young lawyer's mind.

"It is a class action lawsuit."

"That will be fifty dollars."

A voice from behind the lawyer, a man sitting on a stiff wooden bench sounded out, "Cash money."

He looked homeless and alcoholic, his face with a three-day beard was matched by his straggly white hair, unkempt at vast and obtuse angles to his forehead. Frankly the way his hair stood on end, it looked as if the man had been randomly electrocuted.

"I have my credit card of course."

The clerk said gleefully, "Cash money, the county decided not to pay the three percent on credit cards to save for pensions and to help the governor when and where we can."

The voice from behind the lawyer said loudly, "Herman, I already told him that. What are you an echo chamber?"

The clerk simply glared off and behind the lawyer at the man on the bench. He did moderate his tone and remarked somewhat nicely, "That will be fifty dollars...please."

Luckily, because he was not certain, he opened his wallet and with relief the young lawyer took out three Andrew Jackson twenty-dollar bills.

"That will be ten dollars in change," was the sweet return.

The clerk began looking over the filing. "There are some errors here. I can help if you like, or you can simply wait for the rejection notice and then resubmit with another fifty-dollar fee." The young lawyer, fresh out of law school, did have some distant wisp of knowledge from his perspective.

"I quite assure you this would be accepted in the federal court of New York," and then he added disdainfully, "as well as here."

The clerk straightened up, holding the filing out and away from him as if it were a soiled baby's diaper.

"I see here you are citing a tort or civil wrong, based that in the age of time travel, you are claiming that they, specifically time travelers, have done a poor job of running the Earth. And therefore, as claimant representing all humanity past, present, and future you are stating damages because of their egregious and reckless altering of the timeline and hence ipso facto have caused said damages by the inept running of all human affairs. Thus, a class action suit is to be brought forthwith and now in present or future time by said named claimants, specifically all Earth citizens, when and if the first time traveling episode occurs."

"Exactly so."

The lawyer stood straight and tall and added, "Not only that, my dear man, but we are claiming now and in the future, and mind you in the past as well, and plus and asserted doubly therefore in present time, that great harm has been done by the reckless actions taken by the time travelers, et al. And that compensation is hereby claimed by all Earth citizens at large throughout all time." He then added with a slight smile, "For unlimited damages."

"All time specifically or in general?"

"In general."

"Your legal action is hereby accepted this date of…."

A voice boomed throughout the legal chamber. "Wait."

A man walked up the marble stairs who looked exactly like the young lawyer.

The rummy sitting on the bench announced, "Ah twins, isn't that something. It's sort of cute, in its random, quantum physics sort of way."

"I wish to file a counter claim to the unfounded tort action of time traveler recklessness."

The clerk said gleefully, "That's half price because the courts always favor a lively argument."

The young lawyer said, "Wait, I'm not a twin, and that's not fair. I have no idea what is happening here."

The clerk said, "He sure looks like your twin."

The drunken rummy announced, "Twins are always messing with each other, with their teachers, and with the girls they take out on dates. Welcome to the club." The clerk looked at both men suspiciously.

"My counter claim is really very simple. By filing a tort against time travelers this action has created an environment where productivity has dropped, frankly may I say, to near zero. Thus, we are claiming that by suing us, they have damaged the future Earth environment for time travelers at large. We are therefore clearly stating and demanding counter damages, strictly limited to the future, and therefore by definition excluding the past."

The clerk asked dryly, "And you are representing?"

"All time travelers."

The man on the bench said sweetly, "Got ya."

The clerk glared at the drunk, "Vinnie, if you are going to brag around town that you won the bet, I am going to have to ask you to leave. Just because you said you could set a time trap experiment that would draw out and capture the time travelers, et al, and this has happened is no big deal. And it is not the same, nor may I add, nearly as difficult as betting on the Yankees winning the World Series last year, just like I did at ten to one odds."

The young lawyer said only in dismay, "Vinnie Russo?"

The man nodded happily, this time smearing his runny nose with the grimy cusp of his sleeve.

The young lawyer then glared at his future self, who was now his legal opponent.

"You don't stand a chance. I would recommend settling for terms at once."

"No, you don't stand a chance."

The clerk coughed and said loudly, interrupting the two attorneys. "That will be twenty-five dollars."

A voice behind the lawyers bellowed.

"Cash money."

The Game

The Game

Chapter 1

The executive meeting held all the top decision makers. The presentation had been flawless, given by a top manager who had thought the whole idea up. It was as beautiful as a snowflake before it melted into a glob of H_2O and then re-froze into sharp ice.

"I have a problem on several levels."

The woman had spoken up from way down on the far side, designated for the underlings who were allowed to attend and briefly give their thoughts only if their ideas were exceedingly creative and could either make or save money. That end of the table was for the junior vice presidents. The table had enough seats for thirty people as this was one of the largest communication companies on the planet. She was sitting next to a junior VP in charge of finance and on the other side was a junior VP in computer something or other. She was short and stocky, and had the look of a high school English teacher that wouldn't take any guff from anyone. "Primarily the fault lies in that you will be inadvertently running a gigantic experiment without the consent or knowledge of millions of people, and you have absolutely no idea of the unintended consequences."

This idea would not make money. However, it might save money if there were any future legal issues. All eyes turned up the table to the head of legal, senior vice president of a division that contained over a thousand in-house attorneys worldwide. He was a distinguished looking man with graying hair in a wondrous and expensive gray silk suit. He shook his head and began his response.

"Not true on all counts. First, we have announced that we have been slightly speeding up re-run comedy shows for over a year now, to shorten the run time so we could sell more commercial space and make more money. We have not been told of nor have we found any adverse effects whatsoever."

The woman had a look of dismay on her face. "But that's not what you're proposing to do here. You're going to speed up the images of the largest sporting event in the country. Fully one third of Americans are going to tune in, and you will be messing with how their minds perceive reality." This statement would not make money nor would it save money. To everyone in the room it was archaic, almost blasphemous, like swearing in church.

All eyes then turned to the man who had just made the presentation and soon would be promoted to full junior VP status. "We have complete approvals of course. The government has in point of fact requested, for national security issues, to have a time delay. I imagine they got the idea from the Russian Federation when they hosted the Olympics. The entire world was seeing a tape delay. So we comply and why shouldn't we, as a corporation that answers to stockholders, worldwide I might add, why wouldn't we take advantage of this situation? We would be letting our stockholders down if we did not." He paused and then added, "And many of our stockholders have their retirement funds entrusted to our cleverness."

The room fell silent and the soon to be junior vice president continued, "Also if anyone decided to take off their clothing during half-time and run across the field we will be helping defend the union by editing out such abominations, and thus we will protect the sensitivities of little old ladies in Kansas."

There was broad laughter in the room, and someone said, "Or not," and then there was boisterous mirth.

"Wait, stop." The short stocky woman stood up, and the room fell completely silent. She stared up one side of the table and then down the other with a look of disbelief.

"Have you all lost your minds? You are going to feed a false reality to hundreds of millions of people, no billions of people." She paused, desperate to make the point clearly. They had to listen.

Down on the far end of the table the president leaned over to the senior vice president and whispered, "Did she get her termination notice early?"

"No, it's scheduled for Friday. But this is to our advantage, because she is bordering on kicking in the behavior clause in her contract. She may be wrecking her own golden handshake and her forfeited stock options can then be placed in the executive retirement pool."

The president nodded and stared back at the woman, who in his opinion had just shot herself in the foot.

She got the image and the necessary way of explaining the concept. Her face brightened. "You know, you're at the gym and running on the treadmill, and you step off, it feels like the room has slowed down?" She looked around the table for approval.

In silence she studied the business men and women who either had stone faces or shocked faces as this idea was not going to make any money for the company whatsoever. The president spoke up in his deep booming voice from the far side of the table, "Ms. Smith, that will be quite enough."

"Or when you get off a moving ship, the land seems to be rocking back and forth, like you're still on the boat. It's a really strange feeling because your mind has gotten used to the motion of the sea and now you're on land. Some sailors actually get seasick when they step onto shore."

The president shouted, "Ms. Smith," for these thoughts were wasting everyone's time, and therefore now costing the company money.

"Come down from floating above the table, Ms. Smith, we have business to conduct." That was a tasty handoff by the senior vice president.

But Ms. Smith was like a dog with a bone.

"Look, the people that are making money off these wondrous devices are like the captain of the Titanic welcoming us all on board. The glitter, the excitement, but all of human advancement, all of it, rocketry into space, the Golden Gate Bridge, Shakespeare to Einstein, everything we are, was created by our unbound human minds without the aid of computers. We are now using this computer technology in bizarre ways."

She paused and added, "In our case we are speeding up a broadcast while using advanced subliminal digital messaging."

The president, from way down the table, said in a very angry tone, "Ms. Smith, this is clearly insubordination." The senior vice president had a small clever smile on his face. That statement was now on the record as all meetings were recorded.

Ms. Smith looked around the room. Several high ranking officers of the company were taking notes intently. Maybe she had saved the day after all; maybe some of them did get it. She sat down without saying another word.

The vice president of finance was using her notepad to rapidly calculate that Ms. Smith had just cost herself two million dollars in forfeited stock options at the current trading price of fifty-seven dollars a share, and that her specific percentage had increased her own net worth by forty-two thousand dollars.

The vice president of human resources made a notation that Ms. Smith's termination would now be changed to "for cause" and quickly calculated he would earn twenty-two thousand dollars in bonuses.

The vice president of marketing made a notation wondering what would happen if they speeded up the commercials as well? An interesting idea if he could sell it. He drew a big smiley face on his notepad and wrote, "We could sell more commercials." He calculated that if they squeezed in just three more ads he would earn an extra 120,000 dollars in commissions.

Chapter 2

Sam was just six and a latchkey kid. His mom had two jobs, one as a barista at the local coffee shop and then nights as a waitress. She set up the house in an unusual way. The television was programed to run nothing but old style shows. Andy Griffith in Mayberry, The Waltons, that sort of fare. She didn't want her boy to watch anything else for the hours and hours he would spend in front of the screen, so that was the tiny lad's reality for most of the day. She had heard that they were speeding up the programs slightly and stopped to watch, and yes, she could detect that it was faster, but nothing like the "keystone cops" or anything like that, so she dismissed the aberration.

"Your lunch is in the microwave, and remember, all you have to do is push the button and open the door very carefully when the chime goes off." Sam nodded and didn't say anything because he had heard it before. She frowned and said, "Did you hear me?"

"Yes, Mom, I heard you, and they did, too."

Sam pointed to the empty corner of the kitchen.

"Your imaginary friends, what are their names again?"

The boy said, "Nadar and Nemo. I already said that before."

THE GAME

"And Nadar is the mean one and Nemo is the nice one." She turned and waved to the vacant corner of the kitchen.

"They moved, they are over by the stove now."

"Why is it you can see them and I can't, besides that fact that they are imaginary of course."

The smart lad said, "They said something about my mind working on a different time, that's why I can see them."

"Eat your cereal. Mommy will be back for dinner and to tuck you in. Don't open the door and don't answer the phone unless you see it is from me, okay?"

The little boy jammed down his last bite and then parked in front of the television as usual. He heard his mom shut and lock the door.

Nemo looked something like five or six clear plastic lunch bags that fluttered constantly up and down like wings. The entire shape was cylindrical. Nadar hovered over by the television blocking the view. Sam leaned to the left and then finally got up and moved over a few feet. Nadar, the mean one, was completely negative space. That is, he was the outline of what was there and seemed to absorb every bit of light. Sam had once shined a flashlight at him, and the beam seemed to be utterly sucked into darkness. Sam thought the battery was dead, and then would turn the light on his face, and then at Nemo. That was one of the most fun games ever. Nemo was indifferent to the light beam. It would make its clear wings luminous at just the right angle like a rainbow. Nadar, the mean one, looked somewhat like a half-sized ninja dressed completely in black. There were no eyes of course, just a diffused dark area that could be called a head.

THE FOLDINGS

Nemo moved to the television and shooed away Nadar like a bothersome insect so the boy could keep watching his favorite speeded up show. Sam had learned that if he stopped watching for any period of time, he would have trouble seeing both Nadar and Nemo. They would start to fade and then disappear. So Sam figured out early that the best strategy was to bulk up on the television shows first, so he would be able to play the whole afternoon with Nemo and Nadar, as they were much more fun. They had told Sam that they were the generals, the commanders in a great contest.

Chapter 3

The president of the corporation was given the metadata on potential viewership worldwide. This particular event would have over three billion humans tuning in simultaneously, almost one in three people on the planet. An incredible feat of marketing, but of course they had spent the money, time, effort, and a good deal of brain power to create the vibe, the hype.

He had just wrapped up a legal discussion regarding the termination of Ms. Smith for cause: direct insubordination and disruptive behavior. She had violated several clauses in her contract and the company withheld all bonuses and stock options, at least until she completed a battery of physiological examinations. These were conducted by independent professionals of course because of the legal implications; however, the company was their largest client, and the diagnosis always seemed to go the company's way in cases like this.

His secretary walked in and sweetly said, "You have the presidential suite at the game, helicopter transport to private roof access, all the usual amenities and of course the sound system is set up to pipe in both coaches' private strategy conversations so everyone in the suite will know the plays ahead of time if they wish to tune in."

THE FOLDINGS

The president showed a spark of irritation, "Is Hamilton going to be there?"

"Yes, he has accepted and will be arriving by helicopter."

"He always listens in to the com system and then calls some hapless bookie in Vegas to place last minute bets. For the love of Pete, he is the fourth richest man in the world and uses inside info to make a stinking thirty thousand dollars on the side from some schlepp."

There were two invites to the game allowed: one just this once and the other because he was the life of the party no matter where he went, a type of garnish to the meal. He did, however, make a huge amount of money for the company. The first was the manager who had thought up the idea of speeding up television shows a year back. He was nothing special, but his idea, expressed now through "live television" where one in three people on the planet were tuning in, now that was an apex.

The second was the vice president of marketing. He was handsome, smart, and his idea of speeding up the commercials had made the advertisers uneasy. But then, he had convinced them to use the technique to their own advantage. Improve the subliminal messaging appearing behind the commercial images by increasing the frequency. Some data showed they would be more effective, more absorbing, and thus more product units would be sold.

Ms. Smith, who had just been fired, used her credit card at an outdoor recreation store, bought all the camping gear she could find plus thirty days of food and a water filtration kit. She took only one thing from her home: a golden retriever she had named Grisle. The two of them headed for the hills.

The day of the big game, the cities across the globe became still and quiet. It was all a go and everyone was at a party or in their homes. Sports bars were filled to maximum and all televisions at airports, hotel lounges, mobile devices were all turned on. There were the random few people that had to perform critical services and some elderly types walking around. A handful of people had learned that shopping or doing anything they wanted in such a quiet city on such a distracting day was a blessing. Although, secretly those "out of step people" felt a bit odd.

The first call came in about five minutes into the game. A woman had dialed 911 while hiding in her closet. She said she had been watching the game when she noticed a man in her apartment.

She was breathless and scared. She said he looked like a ninja dressed completely in black. Several police cars responded at once. They broke down her door and rescued the hysterical woman. The problem was she stayed that way. She kept pointing to a vacant corner of the room screaming that he was still there and why didn't the police arrest him or do anything and this of course worsened her condition. The medical request was called in but the radio frequency was becoming over used.

There was some sort of riot at the sports bar at the mall; it was feared an active shooter situation had developed. People were running, screaming, and pointing off into space.

A huge passenger plane had been crisscrossing the country. The captain pointed at the city where the big event was in progress 40,000 feet below. "Any updates?" The copilot was watching the game intently on his handheld while the captain was flying, giving verbal play by play. The captain was scanning the gauges and the sky.

Suddenly the copilot screamed, "Terrorist in the cockpit." The captain turned, but there was nothing there. The copilot had gone through the training and was allowed to be armed. He immediately drew his pistol and fired all nine rounds at nothing, but the bullets caused immediate decompression and an electrical fire.

There was a refinery explosion near the game and the massive concussion could not be heard over the joyous shouts of the crowds. They could however see the plume of black smoke, but those things happened sometimes. What changed was when other plumes of black smoke started to rise up from all points on the compass.

Three large and muscular security guards burst into the private suite, grabbing the president of the largest communication company on Earth by both arms and began dragging him to the door. "Sir, there is a situation; your helicopter has been called. This is now a national security issue." As an icon of a number of the largest companies, he was viewed as a national asset. "What's going on?"

"We don't know, but it's worldwide."

The security for the other corporate elites also showed up at the suite as the word got out at the game itself. Panic started as everyone began heading for the exits at once. They had no idea what was happening; they just knew the rest of the world was collapsing around them. On the roof, the president watched as his five million dollar Sikorsky helicopter banked gracefully and slowed for a landing. One of the guards on the deck had been in the security booth on roof level and had actually been watching the game on television. He suddenly screamed, said something like, "They're in the helicopter," took out his .45, and unloaded the entire clip at the Sikorsky. The other security guards were only momentarily confused as they shot the crazy man dead. The five million dollar Sikorsky, however, wasn't worth much after that as it began spinning uncontrollably, slamming into the parking lot below the stadium in a fireball creating complete pandemonium.

The president of the corporation went to the railing and saw nearly a hundred thousand people below all running at once, multiple fires burning across the city, and a giant jumbo jet at remarkably low altitude, which banked suddenly, crashing into a nearby neighborhood.

The nuclear submarine, "Yellowfin," had half the crew watching the game. The ensuing chaos caused the vessel to begin a deep plunging dive. But not before it had launched six of its nineteen nuclear missiles.

Chapter 4

Nadar stopped and looked over at Nemo with its fluttering wings. The boy heard, "It is over, the planet is ours."

Nemo, the galactic referee for such events said, "You have won and played fairly. No physical violence and no introduced viruses. You brought in only positive devices as you claim them to be on your part. They have eliminated themselves as you predicted without a shot fired."

The reply was only, "It is easy to drive lemmings off a cliff."

Nemo seemed sad, its wings darkened and flittered more slowly.

The boy looked at Nemo with concern for he had been listening to the exchange. "Does this mean we can't play anymore?

Nadar said, "Indeed so, little insect"

Sam hesitated and looked at Nemo, "You said you were the general; aren't you the one to decide if we can keep playing?"

Nemo flittered a little sideways, his wings rainbowed up, and he said to Nadar, "I declare a revision."

Nadar immediately said, "Cause?"

"They are not completely destroyed, although the infrastructure they rely so heavily on has been."

Nadar moved close to the boy in a menacing way and said, "Statistically, we calculate a general decline. Small groups will decrease in size and become less capable. The end is inevitable within one hundred years."

Nemo said quickly, "I disagree. This young boy was attached to the electronics only so he could then play with us later in the day. His first choice is to play creatively, no matter how tempting you have made their devices. His first choice is not your way."

Nadar countered, "They only play and are creative in war, all their sports as you call them, are derivatives of combat and self-annihilation. We simply encouraged their own barbaric tendencies."

Nemo said, "Figure skating has no model in warfare, surfing, among many. You speak of the gaming devices you have made so appealing. But I see many still turn their back on such computer play, realizing computers are a fabulous tool like a shovel, and many here do not like to play with shovels. They would all learn this in time."

Nadar said distastefully, "Time is a chimera and these humans are stupid lemmings."

"No, I find they are more akin to clever, watchful small birds. I am officially determining that the outcome is still uncertain. The contest continues."

Upside Down

Upside Down

The meeting was horrific. All the top generals were there, most of the world's top scientists. The President of the United Nations said only in disbelief, "Hundreds of thousands of civilizations conquered without a single defeat."

The man leading the meeting was a nondescript, mid-level United Nations employee; he was the perfect facilitator and hence had been chosen for this job. To be in this particular auditorium, each person was selected because they were the best of the best and included almost every field of human endeavor.

The facilitator continued, "They fold time so they see the entire history of the planet they are going to invade. They know, for example, the military capabilities at the time of the landing, and customize their advanced forces to guarantee victory. And of course in the case of Earth, they know the history of every battle fought, every outcome, every strategy we have ever employed throughout time from Hannibal to Custard. As General Patton would have commented, 'They have read our book.'"

There was stunned silence throughout the auditorium. A voice from the back said, "But why?"

The facilitator coughed. "It's not about good versus evil. Their belief system could best be described as a massive galactic IQ test. They are not invading to seize resources, to conquer. In their view, they are preparing the galaxy for the next challenge, and they believe this sort of natural selection is necessary for the advancement of life in what is obviously a very hostile universe."

The facilitator paused, looking around at the assembled representatives of every nation on Earth. He continued, "In that view, they have announced that any civilization that defeats or causes just one error in their tactical abilities will receive all the cumulative knowledge that they have gained, and all the invading forces, on all those hundreds of thousands of conquered worlds, will destroy themselves immediately. As my grandmother used to say, all we have to do is 'prove they are dumber than a dung beetle' and we only need to do it once."

"What do they do with the citizens of the worlds they...."

"They are viewed as inferior and natural selection demands complete destruction."

"When are they going to arrive?"

"Four years. They are en route with the expeditionary force."

The meeting then began to break down into a type of simmering panic. The room was like a single living creature that found itself going down. People were talking over each other, arguing. One general was saying it was impossible, another was countering that these creatures were complacent with all their assured victories and thus vulnerable. There was talk of building an escape rocket ship for the chosen few. "To go where?" said a loud voice.

The facilitator let this continue—let them get it out of their system.

Finally in a booming voice he said, "They have gone nearly across the entire galaxy, as Earth was luckily located on an outer backwater arm of the furthest spiral from where they started their test. They are faced now with only a handful of civilizations of which the Earth is considered the least advanced of the remaining group."

A good question was brought up. "They are in this meeting then? What I mean is, are they watching even now?"

"No, once en route, they cannot observe what is happening. While in transit they will be completely blind to the nature of light and folding time. Time jumping stops their observational capabilities. Actually, for them the trip is instantaneous. They use biologicals to mark time not star charts as they technically are not going anywhere. It sounds strange but they are waiting for our, or rather the Earth's, singularity to solidify, then their ships will appear." The room settled a bit. This was something at least.

The facilitator took on a much more serious persona. "They have sent this data as a sort of test prep; that's the best analogy."

He then scanned the silent auditorium left to right. "Ideas?"

The look on his face was encouraging. His eyes were alive, transmitting by pure body language that humans were at their best and most dangerous when cornered.

One of the generals began, "Let's begin by seeing what we have and how we can coordinate and work together as one." Discussions began that were useful, but not what the facilitator was looking for.

After a bit of time he said again, more forcefully, "Ideas."

A woman, a famous sculptor, said in return, "What are we best at, what do humans do best?"

There was a general discussion. "Space exploration," was one such idea, but that was shot down at once. "We could get to the moon using visuals, no computers whatsoever, just riding a beefed up Second World War V2 rocket and steering the thing manually. Where is our moon base, our Mars colony? We have been pathetic at space exploration and now we are ill-prepared."

The sculptor spoke up again, "That's not what I'm talking about. Not our achievements, but what we are as humans."

Another woman, a painter famous for color matching said loudly, "Subterfuge." Many people turned to look; the room was silent waiting for more. "We trick our spouses who know us perfectly, we hide things, we secretly read our children's diaries and deny with complete believability. We even deceive ourselves."

The facilitator nodded his approval.

A general spoke up, "We are very good at that, but if they know our military history, they will recognize this trick. They will expect us to have fake bases and command centers. This they will be prepared for."

The painter said, "That's not exactly what I am talking about."

But the room had erupted and was beginning to panic again. Desperate ideas started whirling around. The facilitator stopped this at once.

In a loud voice he said, "Excuse me, if you would finish your thought and please stand." He was pointing at the woman.

She did so, somewhat nervously. Then she did something unexpected. "Let me ask those in the military a question.

If there were a hostage situation by a rogue government, and they said they were going to begin executing the prisoners one by one unless this or that was given to them, what would you do?

One general said, "Helicopter squadron, special forces, night-time rescue."

Another said, "Start invasion preparation, drones, laser bombing, then boots on ground."

Then from a third, "Naval forces...."

The facilitator said, "No, remember they have read your book. They will know all your tac-tics."

He then pointed to the artist like she was queen. "What would you do, madam?"

"I would ask for volunteers and have dozens of cruise ships at the ready. Once they landed all would say, "Take me in place of a hostage." Suddenly, the offending nation would have tens of thousands of people showing up on their shores yelling, "Take me instead. And because this has never been done, and it is not in our history, the space aliens would be completely baffled at a strategy like this."

There was a mood change in the room, one of hope.

The facilitator said with pride, "The unbounded human mind at work."

A general spoke up. "Alexander the Great did the same thing with the siege of Tyre in 332 B.C. The Persians went out on an island fortress to wait out the invading army. That had always worked in the past. Alexander built a causeway to the island; that had never been done before in military history. Of course, that was a big surprise to the Persians."

Everyone turned to the artist. She smiled. "Why don't we throw them a party?"

The facilitator knew it had happened. He could see it in her face, feel it in the room.

"A planet-wide masquerade party, and we act like it's sometime in the past with our costumes, maybe the seventeenth century."

A scientist stood up at once. He was very excited. "They would have to assume their calculations were all wrong. They jumped into the wrong time."

A general said, "Their commander would probably panic, I know I would."

Another scientist said, "They may very well return to their home world at once."

Then someone else said, "They would rework their calculations using the false Earth time. They would think they were in by error and jump back to their planet hundreds of years or more into the wrong time by mistake."

As if from on high, a Nobel Prize winning physicist said, "They would incorrectly return to an early time on their own home world because of this miscalculation." He then added with glee, "Their own timeline would become shredded."

A laureate mathematician said, "They might actually cause themselves to disappear altogether due to time paradoxes."

The facilitator said, "We have four years to pull it off. To tear down skyscrapers, to hide the infrastructure, to make it seem like they have arrived in the wrong time."

The sculptor said, "But right on time for the party."

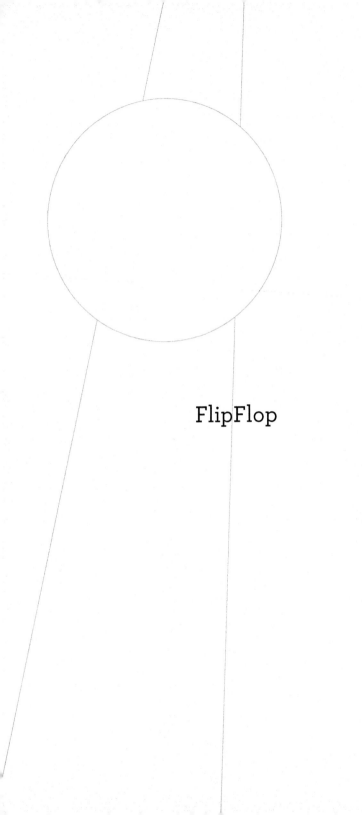

FlipFlop

Chapter 1

Her soft voice said in amazement, "Look at this."

With a conspiratorially deep voice he said, "I've never seen the prices that low; that can't be round trip for two?"

She nodded and said, "We've been waiting for this."

She looked over his shoulder, reading aloud, "As our gift to you, our traveling partners, Princess Interstellar Cruise Lines, wants you to have a very special keepsake. As a reminder of the best time in your life, your Mars' experience, we offer your very own robot as our gift to you."

They both said at the same time, pointing to the ad, "And you get a robot." They laughed at each other, the sort of comfortable laugh of a couple who has been married for almost ten years. Their anniversary was coming up and both were keeping an eye out do something special to celebrate.

The intercom chimed on their home computer system.

"Professor Martin."

"Yes."

A pleasant voice with the perfection achieved only by computers said, "The University HR department requests you schedule your sabbatical with your department head. As a reminder, if you do not use this opportunity for sabbatical time, unlike your vacation credits, it does not accumulate."

Professor Neil Martin was always impulsive. "How much vacation time have I accumulated?"

"Neil, you're not honestly thinking of booking a Mars vacation? The cost is outrageous even with the discount."

"It's for a ten-year anniversary and why not? And we get to keep the robots after all."

His wife was sitting next to him, and she gave him a broad smile. He was always impulsively talking them into outrageous adventures—wine tasting in Chile, parasailing off Costa Rica—and she loved him for it. So her mouth was saying one thing, but her blue eyes sparkled and said something else altogether.

She said, "If we do make the decision to go, and I'm not saying it's a good idea." She had a devilish look of a co-conspirator and added, "I've always wanted to say I learned to ski on Mars."

Waiting for the pause in the conversation the computer said, "Professor Martin, you have accumulated six months of unused vacation and five weeks of medical leave for a total of seven months and one week."

"Neil, really, we can't afford this." She swept back her raven hair, her mouth open in disbelief. She added, "30,000 credits... each."

"Nancy, with my sabbatical time added to my vacation and sick leave...."

"That's not what I'm saying; we can't afford it." And that part was true.

They both ignored the computer from the University HR department, and it chimed to indicate the link had closed.

Neil grinned. "We get the lapel pin and can wear it for life."

Nancy absentmindedly reached up to her collar where a bronze pin with an oak cluster was prominently displayed. The pin telling everyone she had made it to a low Earth orbit of fifty miles high, but the cluster saying she had gone further into a high orbit of over 250 miles. That had been some flight, just a few hours long, but she had been twirling and pushing off walls like Wonder Woman. And then of course she had gotten all the free stuff with the pin.

Being allowed to wear the pin was by Presidential Order. And it was impossible to counterfeit as the hologram was linked to the bio signature of the wearer.

She had secretly hoped that one day she would have a lunar pin. You hardly ever saw someone with one of those. And a Mars pin, the coveted red, telling all her friends....

Neil said, "We got pretty good free stuff with our high orbit pin, but with the Mars pin...even more."

He let that part trail off. Because indeed part of the benefit of supporting space discovery was bragging rights and cool free stuff. Companies across the planet supported the mission. The high orbit pin had bought lifetime free coffee from Starbucks.

Neil could see his wife wavering. "Look what we get with the Mars pin. The advertisement shows these in small print, 'Automatic room upgrade on any Hilton property. Lifetime MVP Gold status on Alaska Airlines'—Oh, and Amazon gives you free shipping for life. And here, half off on a new Tesla and here from Virgin Atlantic....." And the list went on and on.

"Okay, Neil, what is all this stuff really worth?"

"Let's add it up and see."

Neil went into his scientific mode. "The robot is the big item. It's worth 3000 credits and that's times two since we each get one."

"But I wouldn't sell mine."

Neil was perplexed. "Why not?"

"Look, you can see why they are giving you the robot. They have designed it deliberately to match our form, so they look more like us." She was pointing to the ad and right there on the robot's shoulder was the Mars territorial flag. By law only something that had been to Mars could wear the flag.

"It's free advertising for Princess Interstellar Cruise Lines because when I go to the store, I have my personal assistant, my robot with the flag. It makes it more than the pin, it's even better." Neil did what he had always done time and again in their marriage. He said in a low tone, "Okay, what if we just sell my robot then?"

She nodded and she reached over and held his hand. "But Neil we still can't afford it, and you would want to keep your robot wouldn't you?"

"I get free use of the University bot." He looked over in the corner at a highly shared, older model robot used by all the teachers in the physics department.

Nancy said, noticing the chipped paint on the three-foot-high droid, "They need to upgrade their pool of bots."

"Yes, but it's free."

Nancy was now fully onto the idea of going to Mars. "I can take a leave of absence from my job in the emergency room."

FLIP FLOP

"They give us each a Rolex designed for space."

Nancy said, "That's worth a thousand credits."

Neil responded, "That I am not going to sell, I refuse."

They finally agreed that it was an adventure first, and anniversary gift to each other second.

Neil said, "It's once in a lifetime." They would have to take out a loan and drain both of their savings, but they were going to Mars.

They shook hands with each other and said at the same time said, "Deal."

Chapter 2

The concierge was dressed in a blue jumpsuit. He had dark hair and was very athletic looking with a perfect smile.

"Mr. and Ms. Martin, welcome to the first step of your travel adventure on Princess Interstellar Cruise Lines."

Nancy was beaming with delight. "Are we going to meet our robots today?"

The man looked down at his computer screen, "Yes, once all your fellow shipmates have arrived."

They were at a modern space port in the Nevada desert to board the rocket shuttle that would deliver them to the cruise ship currently in stationary high orbit.

The concierge smiled. "Our launch window confirmed departure is in two hours; we have you both checked in and the lounge is just down the hall. Welcome."

The spacious MVP admiral's club was comfortable and almost all the passengers had arrived.

The passenger manifest was sixty tourists; most were couples because being a single in a cabin doubled the price. But there were a few cabins allocated for these high rollers.

The cruise also featured two pilots and a crew of twenty to cater to every whim.

Among these crew members were specialists in many fields. Because the cruise lasted for slightly over six months, most of the passengers had decided to have fun learning a new hobby. A new language, specialty cooking, and even landscape painting—something Mars was known for.

The two cruise directors stood before the group. A handsome man and a gorgeous woman.

"Hello, soon to be fellow Martians." There was applause all around. "We are here to help with any questions, and mostly over the next six months we are here simply to make sure you have the time of your life."

The passengers were of all ages. Some were on vacation, some were on business, while others were retired and seeing the inner planetary system for themselves.

The woman said, "My name is Jane Sellwood. And my partner in this endeavor to make sure you have nothing but fun is Sam Heartwood." She added, "Of course these cruises are known for their fabulous meals prepared by our professional Cordon Bleu chefs." She pointed to four of the crew, who stood up and took bows.

Sam said, "And it's expected you're going to gain some mass."

Jane added, "But gravity on Mars reduces that by two thirds, so eat as much as you like."

This brought on more applause.

Nancy leaned over to Neil and said, "I hope not too much."

Sam said, "The average gain is two pounds a month, so you're each going to put on about twelve pounds."

Neil looked at Nancy with mock horror. "It will be a torture, won't it?" The computer coffee table where they were seated had the menus from the three onboard restaurants.

The concierge said, "We really don't want you to gain too much as your personal robot must increase its mass in exactly the same way." He paused pointing to his stomach and then to his backside, "and in the same places." Then he added, "But it doesn't make them suffer like us."

The group was snickering and enjoying themselves when an older man with graying sideburns and a younger woman walked in. They had silver epaulettes and astronaut wings.

The cruise directors both beamed. "Oh yes, here is your flight crew. Let me introduce your pilot, Captain Steve Simms and his copilot, Commander Joanna Harper." Sam continued, "If you all would come with me to the conference room we can meet your personal robots. You will be keeping them after the cruise as our personal gift to you."

Joanna Harper, the copilot, was lovely and a perfect match to the very handsome captain.

Following behind, Neil gave Nancy a look that said, "This is going to be great."

They all walked to a large atrium and in the center was a model of the cruise ship about three meters long. The captain said, "May I present to you, the Da Vinci."

The holographic image rotated and then cut the ship in half so the interior compartments were displayed with small computer generated people enjoying various activities. Of course the passengers had seen all this before on their own computers, but now they were being given a personal visual tour.

Commander Harper was standing in front of a three-dimensional hologram of the ship. She was explaining the compartments and how life aboard a luxury space cruiser would operate. She pointed, "As you can see the ship rotates around its central axis. The pods are the outside of the 'wheel' with the spokes; these passageways connect to the center segment."

Neil said, "You spin the ship so there is artificial gravity."

Captain Simms said, "Exactly, and we set the spin rate at first to duplicate Earth's gravity, but over time we begin to gradually reduce the spin to duplicate the gravity on Mars. You won't even be aware it's happening. Then when you step off the ship, the one third gravity on Mars feels completely normal. Then of course we repeat the process going back to Earth." He had perfect teeth with a grand smile and he said, "Of course when you step off at Earth you are completely acclimated and can go right out that very day and play a round of golf."

Commander Harper said, "And you're going to need to after your weight gain."

Everyone clapped and laughed and someone from the group said, "This is going to be the best."

The captain said, "Any questions?"

One of a frumpy looking couple in their late fifties said, "Do we have to know how to operate anything?"

Commander Harper said, "Not a thing. Flying the ship is up to us. We will show you some basic safety protocols; however, these are really very simple."

Nancy said, "I can see these pods opposite from our cabin, and they look exactly the same."

The captain nodded, "Those pods are for your robots. We call them your 'self-similars.'"

The three dimensional model spun and enlarged so images of robots could be seen in their compartments.

The captain looked over at Joanna Harper and said, "You wanna take it this time?" They were both used to explaining this phase over and over.

"Sure, I've got it."

The model spun so that in the human pods were representations of tiny people, walking, cooking dinner.

"As you know you have your own kitchens and your pods are large, 800 square feet. Just like your home, you will be walking around, and that shifts mass."

Then Joanna continued, "We call your pods 'homes,' because really they are more akin to a small condominium with a living room and separate bedroom. You won't have windows; we found the spinning is disconcerting visually. But any wall you choose gives you the view electronically without the rotation with the computer readjusting the actual image. It's really spectacular when we're near Mars. The red planet looming ahead." She shook her head in disbelief with a beautiful smile

Nancy pointed, "What are these areas on the ship?"

"The center portion of the ship is the 'play rooms.' Here of course there is no gravity, and we have designed rooms for different events. We are going to teach you the most amazing games you have seen in your life. And if you like we can pair up on teams, all the better. There is nothing more fun than playing sports in space. Everyone is a champion."

The captain looked at his watch. "It's time for you to meet your robots." And with that a side door opened and there was a row of robots. They had the exact form of the person they were built to copy. Some were tall, some short. One man from Texas had a pot belly and his robot had the same.

He said in a Texas drawl, pointing to the robot's copious belly, "Do you think you could have left that part out...for both our sakes?"

The captain said smiling, "Okay, everyone stand in front of your robot." Besides having the same body shape they had a name painted on their white frames in black. Neil found himself in front of Neil 2, his self-similar.

The robot had the shape of a human but with no eyes. Humans had found them disconcerting, although manufacturers had tried time and again to sell the idea. Eyes were hard to duplicate and the best efforts produced a glassy stare from the robots that humans found creepy.

The robots used internal radar accentuated with high frequency sound waves out of the range of human hearing to determine their position in space time. The bots were also linked to wire sensors embedded in the floors of the rooms.

The captain said, "Now as you are probably aware, space flight to Mars on a commercial basis became viable only after we solved the gravity problem with the advancements in robotic technology."

Joanna said, "Spinning the spaceship actually stabilizes the craft, the same reason rifling is used in the barrel to create spin on the bullets."

Steve added, "One problem with spinning spaceships, though, is people move around, and that changes the center of mass and creates new stability issues. And just like the tire on your car, if it goes out of balance you get a vibration. We spin the spacecraft to create artificial gravity, but as soon as someone moved, changed the center of mass, the ship would start to wobble."

Joanna said, "Steve, do you remember those first flights with the primitive self-similar robots?"

The captain smiled and nodded, "I sure do. Those early bots could only copy our movements if we walked in slow motion. To cross the cabin took ten minutes. But it was worth it to have the gravity. Life is just better that way. Now of course, these next generation bots can even anticipate your motions. They do this by analyzing your stride and habit patterns. So if you want to skip across your compartment, our detection webbing senses your balance has shifted and those signals are sent to the bot. So you have complete freedom of motion."

Joanna said, "I've activated your bots, and this conference room has the same sensor webbing as the ship, so give it a go."

Neil raised his hand and the bot did exactly the same thing. He stepped back, and it seemed like he was looking into a mirror. The bot stepped back. He stood on one leg and then hopped on one leg. With perfect timing the Neil 2 did the same exact thing, in exactly the same way.

Chapter 3

Nancy said, "We will be docking on Mars in three months, halfway there." She was sitting on the couch of their unit and added, "Neil, we should start signing up for the terrestrial activities. Just look at this list. High altitude glider lessons, skiing on carbon dioxide, spelunking." Then she said, "Oh, the Smiths have invited us over to their place for dinner Friday night and then a game of bridge. Sam wants to show off his sushi making skills."

Neil was at his desk and said distractedly, "Yeah, that sounds fine."

Nancy had taken up Spanish, and most everyone had dived into one avocation or another.

Back on Earth the conversation would go something like this, "Yes, I learned how to make a fine sushi meal on my way to Mars." Then the inevitable question, "You went to Mars?" and the smug response, "The best experience of my life."

Neil had decided to learn robotics. To become an expert. It would look good on his resume at the University, but more importantly he was simply curious about something that would copy his every movement for a total of a year, six months over and six months back. He realized that in the opposite pod Neil

2 was sitting at a desk exactly like his, keying into a computer that wasn't hooked up to anything.

He stood and went to the kitchen, grabbed a glass and filled it with water at the sink. Neil 2 did exactly the same thing in exactly the same way. Including drinking the water so his mass would match. For solid food weight, Neil 2 still consumed liquid, just of a slightly higher density; while human Neil might be enjoying a perfectly cooked filet, Neil 2 used a feeding tube.

Neil said, "You know the secret, why they're giving us these bots, is that they are over-specialized."

He looked over at Nancy, who was at her desk using social media to connect to her friends on Earth. She nodded absent-mindedly, but she wasn't really paying attention. Robots were all Neil talked about now.

He motored on, "So the cruise line really can't reuse them, and we won't be able to sell them, either, unfortunately."

Nancy said distractedly, "We can make up the 3000 credits someplace else, maybe on Mars. We won't go to Mount Vasivous. We can cancel that part and stay around Mars City."

Neil said, "The only thing those bots will be good for is standing in the corner of our house, and maybe I will put lamp shades on their heads."

Nancy laughed, "Well, they have the flag of Mars painted on them. It's colorful." The flag was important as it had been designed and agreed upon before anyone had been to Mars. On landing, it was a symbol of unity and when placed in the ground next to the first footprints just about everyone on Earth thought, "Hey, that's nice; it's not a flag of a specific country but of all of our efforts."

Neil set down his glass and turned. Neil 2 on a pod rotating on the opposite spoke of the wheel a hundred yards away did the same thing.

Then Neil took a step to go back to his desk and Neil 2 didn't. The bot just stood there.

The alarm went off immediately.

Nancy said, "What's that?" with a bit of fear on her face.

Neil said, "That's the signal that our robots have a failure."

Within seconds, on the wall that had a fabulous electronic view of deep space, the million stars suddenly became the huge face of Captain Simms.

"Ah, Neil, Nancy, I'm going to ask you not to move for a moment, just stay in place."

Nancy said, "Steve, what's going on?"

The captain's face was relaxed. He had practiced this emergency time and again. "Neil's robot has malfunctioned, and we are asking you to remain stationary as well just in case it's the floor webbing that's causing the anomaly. If that's true then your bot, Nancy 2, will malfunction as well. Should be just a few moments to work this out. We already have a replacement bot on its way from central storage."

The captain's face disappeared, and the view returned to deep space.

Neil shrugged, and Nancy stayed at her desk.

After a few moments the captain's voice came over the intercom, "Ah, Neil, if you would take one step forward on my mark. Three, two, one...step."

Neil took one step, and there was no alarm. The captain's face appeared on the wall. "Your bot's back to normal; you can both move normally." Anticipating the question the captain said, "Sometimes we get these hiccups is what I like to call them. On their own the bots initiate a diagnostic, and that cures it ninety-nine percent of the time. I'm recalling the replacement bot and good old Neil 2 is back on the time clock."

Then the captain said, because really he was more of a cruise director than a captain most of the time, "Neil, I know you're studying robots so I will send you the full report on the malfunction if you would like to see it."

"Steve, I absolutely would."

The captain nodded, "More code than I would ever care to look at, but you're welcome to it." Then he added, "You're one up on me in weightless basketball—you wanna meet over at the court in an hour so I can even up the score?"

Neil said, "Our usual bet?"

"You got it."

When they were playing basketball the captain's self-similar bot and Neil's bot simply moved to a storage compartment in the center of the ship and waited. Only on the rapidly swinging outer pods was mass equivalency mandatory.

That night, Neil snuggled up to Nancy in bed. She said, "What's your bet with the captain anyway?"

Neil smiled, "I get an extra spacewalk."

"No, you don't." Nancy raised herself up with a smile.

"The captain said I could come with him to do an inspection of the external communication center."

Spacewalks were loathed by the insurance company, because there was an extra element of risk. It took time to train the passengers how to use the spacesuits; passengers were tested and practiced in a center compartment specifically designed for the purpose. It was exactly like when someone went to a hotel and got a scuba diving rating during an Hawaiian vacation. And now Neil was going to get an extra open ocean dive so to speak.

Of course the certification of spacewalking would mean the red Martian pin would have a diamond cluster. About half the passengers took up the challenge.

Neil leaned over and kissed Nancy. "And if I keep winning at weightless one on one basketball, I will get more spacewalks and that means an eventual signoff."

Nancy said with glee, "Fancy you, my husband who will be a part-time space pilot." Neil affectionately brushed some of Nancy's hair away from her forehead. On the opposite pod his self-similar robot was doing exactly the same thing to Nancy 2, but of course there was no hair. "I still have this strange image in my mind of our robots in their bed together looking into what...their sensor units?"

Neil said, "I know, I try not to think about it."

Chapter 4

Over the length of the voyage the captain became good friends with Neil. They played sports together; space fencing was the captain's favorite. A gravity variation allowed one opponent to be upside down while parrying. Neil took not only his third, but fourth and fifth spacewalks.

He was sent the codes regarding the malfunction of Neil 2 and what had overloaded the circuits was the new, "anticipation" aspect of the CPU. Neil was reluctant to do so—he wasn't officially an expert in robotics—but during a card game he expressed his concerns to the captain.

"My deal." Neil began shuffling and said, "I think there is something more going on with Neil 2 than a simple reboot. I believe the bot might start to be—well, I am just going to say it—sentient."

Steve scoffed at this idea. "We have been looking for signs of that for decades in all the robots on Earth. Remember those terrifying science fiction stories, those dreadful movies that robots would view humans as a threat and exterminate all of us?" Then he added while looking at his cards, "And obviously we are all still here talking about it."

Neil said, "Look here." He then turned on the computer that was also the table top for the card game. The computer sensed where items were placed and accounted for the blocked areas.

"See this code streaming? A huge amount of storage was occupied in about a nanosecond by Neil 2 during his malfunction."

Steve said, "Of course, they are programmed to include data points to add the anticipation of our actions. This can be complex. Humans are habitual; the robots are designed to be perfect imitators. That is what they are built to do."

Steve waved his hand over a part of the table, and there was a camera shot of his robot playing invisible cards with Neil 2. Steve waved his hand over one part of the table to magnify, and his robot waved exactly the same way. The robots' table did not have a built-in computer and was a bland steel gray color.

Steve said, "It's a perfect pantomime and nothing more."

The next day, Steve, who had a wicked sense of humor, sent Neil a message. Specific cuts from the movie, 2001: A Space Odyssey. When Neil called up to the bridge instead of Neil's voice Steve got a recording playing the song Daisy.

Neil laughed and said, "Clever bastard," in the message delivery system.

Neil kept studying up on robotics. One day after a fine breakfast he said, "I think this code storm, that's what I am calling it, has an analogy. For us, we would say the lightbulb went off. I think that's why Neil 2 malfunctioned."

Nancy had been listening to this line of reasoning for over a month. "That's nice, dear. The Minkoskeis have invited us over for dinner. Judy says she wants to test her latest pastry dish on us, and Bob wants to practice up on his French. He says he has set the computer to use corrections by translating his French into English. He's on his own for the entire night and can't ask for anything unless it's in correct and proper French or the computer won't be able to translate for us."

Neil was at his desk studying real time code inputs that Neil 2 was using. He could see the low energy use, not much happening. And then there was a spike. Lots of CPU storage coming online. He said, "There it goes again. Not as much as last time, but huge, beyond the normal requirements." Neil got up to go to the kitchen.

The alarm went off. Walking across the living room, Nancy stopped and said, "Not again."

The captain's face appeared, shaking his head. "Sorry about this, folks, same drill as last time. Yes, it's Neil's bot again."

Nancy said, "Neil, I think you should just have the replacement bot sent no matter what. The company doesn't want to do that because it costs them money. But this is ridiculous." She was standing with her hands on her hips. "Neil, are you listening to me? Neil?"

Neil was staring at his monitor, his mouth open wide. He was reading the message in large letters across the screen at his desk. It was from Neil 2. It said, "I step first now."

Chapter 5

"What? How?" was sent across the solar system to every scientist and governmental agency from the moons of Jupiter to the Mercury solar weather station.

Earth's top scientists, the military, and the politicians all went completely nuts. There was wild talk of immediately shutting off any computers that had the possibility of becoming sentient. The dismal reply, "We can't, the dependency would create its own self prophesy of doom. The world, no, the whole solar system's economy would collapse."

The response, "What about just those on the cruise ship?"

The cold answer, "They tried that and bringing up the replacement bots. Any action on the crew's part results in a complete halt by the other self-similar robots. They all go on strike so to speak. If the crew does nothing only the robot called 'Neil 2' is in rebellion."

One of the commanders in the room said, "Jesus, those cruise passengers are being extorted."

Someone else in the room said, "We all are."

Neil was miserable and depressed. The captain had given him only two choices. "You can either stay in one of the center compartments of the ship in zero G's, floating around for the remainder of the cruise, or you can stay in the bathroom of your cabin."

"What? The bathroom?"

"Without your bot matching move for move, walking across your cabin will require us to use the stabilizing jets time and again. We can do that for short periods, but they weren't designed for prolonged duration burns. The ship will run out of solid propellant. We have calculated that if your movements are restricted to the bathroom, we can compensate and have enough maneuvering fuel to satisfy our safety margins."

"Steve, if I spend two months in zero gravity my entire vacation time on the surface of Mars will be ruined as my muscles will need recovery at the hospital."

Neil was sitting on the toilet when Nancy brought him a tray with his dinner. She said, "At least the company is offering us both a full refund."

He just glared. "Thanks for dinner." He added, "You're going out tonight?"

"Yes, it's a ship-wide formal dinner in the main dining pod. Four courses and then some instructions on how to ski with one third gravity. At least by staying here you can do that when we land."

"How lovely."

Neil looked at his world. He had every portable computer he could lay his hands on, even regular paper with notes stuck on the mirror. The problem of Neil 2 could be solved, he just knew it. There was always a way out.

He turned on the monitor and studied Neil 2. The robot was taking an "air step" with his right foot. Up, out, and not touching the ground. The bot looked like a flamingo standing on one leg. A robot that had turned into a broken record, the same movement over and over.

That's when the lightbulb went off in Neil's head. He hit switches and brought up the schematic for the sensor array on the bots. Neil said, "That's it." It took him two days to refine his theory. If anyone had been watching they would have seen his energy levels spike.

On the screen, Steve looked worried. He said, "Neil, this whole weirdness with the bots is best left to the experts. We are going to be landing on Mars in just three weeks now."

Neil shook his head. "No, they don't get it. The robot is sentient, but it doesn't think like we do."

"How so?" was the cold reply.

"We've always thought that robots would exterminate us, because that's what we would do. That is what we have done with competing human groups. We use a type of transference based on how we perceive the universe and then we credit those thoughts to the other sentients."

Steve said in a low tone, "And these robots have proven just that, and by the by, that's why you're stuck in a restroom. It's a miracle this bot mutiny has apparently not spread anywhere else in the system. It's unique to Neil 2 and these ship-based bots."

Neil was shaking his head, "That's not what I'm saying. Because of the nature of light, our main source of information is the photon. Thus that's how we perceive our dimensional space, the delay being critical. But for robots the collection of data points is different. Their main source, their universe as they perceive it, is primarily based on the electron. It's opposite from us. Light hits something and bounces off and we record the data. The bots feed off the electrons, and thus they perceive their dimensional space differently. The bots have an entirely unique perspective. What is important to us, with near certainty will be almost meaningless to them. I'm not saying that's any safer for us, it's just different is all."

Neil added, "Perhaps we are not even perceived by them, so it becomes more of a hypothetical. As an example, how we try to view the eighth dimension in our minds. Very hard to do. Human existence may be a theoretical construct on their part. Hence why it took so long for them to communicate with us in the first place. My theory is that by them copying our every move they didn't become more human, but they began to analyze how we perceive our three-dimensional space."

Steve said, "And then they came up with a model that says hypothetically sentient beings may be occupying three-dimensional space?"

"Something like that, but there is more going on here; I just can't put my finger on it."

Steve gave a heavy sigh. "Well, there is no way to test your theory, and once we are on Mars they will take these bots apart piece by piece and analyze the problem. I can tell you this; never will they be allowed to take over ships again. Especially my ship."

Neil came to a decision. "Monitor my actions. If I'm correct, you're going to get some show."

"Neil, what are you doing?" Then forcefully, "Neil, I order you to halt."

But it was too late. Neil had stood and walked out of the bathroom. The balance alarm started going off, and he ignored it. He could hear the gentle whooshing sound of the chemical jets firing off to balance his pod.

He turned on the switches bringing up the video feed from the Neil 2 pod. He set it so it was on every screen in his unit including the giant wall screens. Neil walked over and then assumed the exact position of Neil 2. They both stood a moment with one leg in the air. Then the captain, who was observing all of this, couldn't believe his eyes. Neil 2 had taken a step, and Neil did the same. And then another, and another, and Neil was imitating the robot. Then Neil 2 was walking in ever decreasing squares around the pod of his living room, followed by the human Neil. Then it started over.

The live feed went to Earth, and scientists across the planet huddled around crowded monitors.

"My God, they are communicating in a new way."

"Look how the bot starts him over in the same position with the foot in the air."

Then from someone else, "There is a slight speed change on that one corner."

Someone else said, "Is anyone counting the number of steps?"

The cruise ship was using its solid fuel rockets to maintain the balance because Neil could not match perfectly, but they were hardly firing.

Across the system, it was viewed by all the scientists as a new communication. And everyone realized it was a fabulous first communication, because it was coming from a sentient robot, and they marveled.

The speaker in Neil's cabin directly linked to Earth. "Professor Martin, are you counting your steps?"

Neil said, "Yes, and if I'm right, the next sequence will be backward to demonstrate time reversal." Neil was right and awkwardly began walking backward to imitate the bot. Finally it ended where it started with the bot standing with his foot in the air and Neil doing the same. But this time the robot held its position. A message came up on all the screens. A picture of an ear and then the question, "Data received?"

A scientist said, "Neil, why not just use the monitor to communicate?"

"If I'm correct they are not sure that method is working. It's obvious to us but only hypothetical to them. They communicate using dimensional space and symbols."

"So, Neil, they are reaching out for a first contact?"

Neil announced, "No, it's more than that. Dimensional space by definition has layers, and so this communication has many elements nested one inside the other." He added, "They are trying to free us. It's all about dimensional space and how those spaces interact and are perceived by sentients in those theoretical domains."

He took a step and Neil 2 followed exactly back to normal. But Neil had gotten the communication.

Earth said, "From what, by what?"

"If I'm right the bots are trying to warn us of something. They perceive data points in the universe we can't see."

Neil's face lighted up. Observational wave collapse gave him the ability to see where everyone else up until now had been blind. He announced, "There is a mirrored dimension."

"Of whom?"

"Of the opposite us, and it's right below our feet, and they have been telling us where to walk step by step. We are dealing with three sentient events. Us, the bots, and something else because our robots have perceived this reality and given us a heads up."

From Earth, "There is something else out there?"

"And I am now going to try and communicate with them."

Neil walked to the desk and taking a piece of paper he wrote backwards using cursive. He then scanned his note on the computer.

It said, written backwards, "I step first now."

CPSIA information can be obtained
at www.ICGtesting.com
Printed in the USA
LVOW06*2008311017

554511LV00015B/63/P